MW00629104

The Bridge of San Luis Rey

Adapted by
David Greenspan

From the novel by
Thornton Wilder

ISBN 978-0-573-70946-3

www.concordtheatricals.com
www.concordtheatricals.co.uk

FOR PRODUCTION INQUIRIES

UNITED STATES AND CANADA
info@concordtheatricals.com
1-866-979-0447

UNITED KINGDOM AND EUROPE
abr@alanbrodie.com
020-7253-6226

Each title is subject to availability from Concord Theatricals Corp., depending upon country of performance. Please be aware that *THE BRIDGE OF SAN LUIS REY* may not be licensed by Concord Theatricals Corp. in your territory. Professional and amateur producers should contact the nearest Concord Theatricals Corp. office or licensing partner to verify availability.

MUSIC AND THIRD-PARTY MATERIALS USE NOTE

IMPORTANT BILLING AND CREDIT REQUIREMENTS

THE BRIDGE OF SAN LUIS REY was commissioned, developed, and first produced by Two River Theater (John Dias, Artistic Director; Michael Hurst, Managing Director) in Red Bank, New Jersey on February 17, 2018. The performance was directed by Ken Rus Schmoll, with sets by Antje Ellerman, light by Yuki Nakase, and costumes by Elizabeth Clancy. The production stage manager was Megan Smith. The cast was as follows:

UNCLE PIO	David Greenspan
DOÑA MARÍA	Mary Lou Rosato
DOÑA CLARA	Madeline Wise
PEPITA	Sumaya Bouhbal
MADRE MARÍA DEL PILAR	Julienne Hanzelka Kim
ESTEBAN	Zachary Infante
MANUEL	Bradley James Tejeda
CAMILA PERICHOLE	Elizabeth Ramos
DON ANDRÉS DE RIBERA / CAPTAIN ALVARADO / DON VICENTE / JAIME / INEZ	Steven Rattazzi

CHARACTERS

UNCLE PIO

DOÑA MARÍA – Marquesa de Montemayor

DOÑA CLARA – Condesa d'Abuirre, Doña María's daughter

PEPITA – young protégé of Madre María del Pilar, servant to Doña María

MADRE MARÍA DEL PILAR – Abbess of Convent Santa María Rosa de las Rosas

ESTEBAN – a scribe

MANUEL – a scribe – Esteban's twin brother

CAMILA PERICHOLE – celebrated Peruvian actress

DON ANDRÉS DE RIBERA – Viceroy of Peru

CAPTAIN ALVARADO – a ship captain

DON VICENTE – Conde d'Abuirre, Doña Clara's husband

JAIME – Camila's son

INEZ – a novice at the convent

SETTING

Peru

TIME

1714

AUTHOR'S NOTES

A sparsely furnished stage is preferable. Characters may remain visible throughout. One actor plays Don Andrés, Captain Alvarado, Don Vicente and Inez – and additionally with the use of a puppet, represent Jaime. He also plays the Camila's "silent" stage partner in the theater sequence.

It is understood that physical action indicated in narrative passages are synchronized with the physical action described.

The rhymes in the verse sections are apparent. Actors should be sensitive to rhyme embedded in the prose.

Uncle Pio acts as stage manager, moving moves set pieces to change the scenes.

UNCLE PIO. Good evening – welcome. We're very happy you're here. We'll get started in just a moment. But before we do may we ask you, if you haven't already, to take a moment to silence your cellphones. That would be very much appreciated. Our play runs about an hour-and-a-half – and we'll perform it without intermission. And we certainly hope you enjoy it.

Now you're going to have to imagine that this is Peru. This bare (for now) stage, Peru. And the play you're about to see is based on Thornton Wilder's book *The Bridge of San Luis Rey.*

It's like I said it's set in Peru – Lima, for the most part – the year is 1714 – July 20th to be exact – it's Noon – and the great bridge of San Luis Rey – a mere ladder of thin slats swung by the Incas a century before over a gorge on the highroad between Lima and Cuzco – well, it just breaks, casting five travelers into the awaiting chasm.

But you'll have to imagine that – now – and at three points later in the play – because we are not dragging out some huge set piece of a bridge onto the stage – for heaven's sake – and having actors doing god knows what – like you'll believe they're falling off a bridge? I think not.

Now it just so happens that at the very moment by the way I'm that strange man you'll come to know as Uncle Pio. Strange some say and disreputable – because... well I work in the theater – I'm a stage director – and for the purpose of our play a sort of stage manager. And needless to say there are those who find contemptible those of us who work in the theater.

I'm also (even worse) an actor who's taken on the *role* of Uncle Pio. And I'm the adapter (of the book). So any fault you find with the play is mine and mine alone.

Now *if* at the very moment the bridge you see in your mind's eye snaps and flings the five gesticulating ants into the valley below you yourself should happen by and stop to wipe your brow and gaze in peace upon the screen of snowy peaks – and then upon the bridge gently swaying and then a twang and then the bridge divides – might you not say to yourself *Oh God!*

Or perhaps you might say to yourself *Thank God!* Within ten minutes I myself would have been on that bridge... I myself... And then perhaps another thought visits your brain: *Why did this happen to those five?*

Five gesticulating ants
into the valley below.
Five souls precipitated.
Five travelers
into the gulf below.

And you wonder what is meant by this catastrophe – an accident or an act of God? Either we live by accident or we don't. You either Believe or you won't. And so you set about to compare the *secret lives* of those five souls this minute falling through the air – determined to make plain why one lives why one dies – why some fall why some rise.

But as memories are hazy – and facts lazily conveyed the volume you fashion never truly captures the central passion of those that fell with the bridge and those that survived them – of Esteban and Manuel the Abbess Madre, Pepita, Camila Perichole, Doña Clara, Don Vicente, Doña María and Uncle Pio – those that lived and those that fell. It is *my* job to tell.

(**DOÑA MARÍA** *seated writing a letter.* **DOÑA CLARA** *stands apart, reading the letter* – **DON**

VICENTE *at his wife's side. On the words*
"crushed" and "crushes" DOÑA CLARA *crushes*
a page of the letter, lets it falls. DON VICENTE
picks it up, smooths the page, reads it.)

Behold: an old woman sitting on her balcony – straw
hat casting a purple shadow across her lined and
yellowed face – a face crinkled like the pages of a letter
crushed by an impatient reader (a pampered beauty
the letter makes furious.) then smoothed by the hand
of one more curious. Yet the paper retains the creases –
like the wrinkled features of an old woman sitting on
her balcony writing a letter to her daughter in Spain –
a daughter so disgusted by her mother's dispatches she
bristles – crushes the letter – leaves it for her husband
who digests its every word its every phrase – relishing
its style – so deserving of praise – preserving his
mother-in-law's epistles. Such a woman is Doña María,
The Marquesa de Montemayor. The laughingstock of
all Lima.

DOÑA MARÍA. My childhood was unhappy,
    I was ugly, I stuttered.
    My mother tormented me
    for she meant for me to have social charms.
    She forced me to walk around town –
    (How people would talk!)
    to promenade
    in some ridiculous gown.
    And a harness of jewels
    draped over my arms.
    Through the streets I fluttered
    like a fool on parade.
    Through the cluttered streets –
    what a fool was I made.
    She sought me a husband –
    I declined them all –
    refined as they all were.

My reticence incensed her.
Hysterical scenes and accusations,
slamming of doors, recriminations.
At last I capitulated to an intellectual ruin –
humiliated – but soon
a daughter was born to me,
a precious jewel.
I fastened my love to her.
I was again made fool.
As she grew she hated me, she berated me
for my speech, for how I dressed –
she took after her father
who heaven be blessed
pre-deceased me. Still –

DOÑA CLARA. *(Holding an as yet crumpled page of the letter.)* My mother tormented me
with her affections –
tortured me with her confections
of love. My rejections
only made her more bold.
Her attempts to hold me were endless.

DOÑA MARÍA. Again and again
hysterical roars –

DOÑA CLARA.
Accusations –

DOÑA MARÍA.
Recriminations,

and the slamming of doors. / and the slamming of doors.

From the offers of
marriage to which
I was subjected I selected one
that expected one's
removal to Spain. Three months
to receive a letter,
three months and so much the better,

three months more
before she gets her reply which means
three months more
before I pick up my pen
and reply to her missives again.

DOÑA MARÍA. The knowledge that love never returns to
me burns at my belief in everything. In everything.
Still I persist in my notes to her.
To still my pain I write to her,
contrite to give her pleasure –
my treasure in Spain,
describing life in Lima as divertingly as I may.

And today my love to the theatre I go,
with Pepita, my love,
to the theatre, my love,
which I know, my love, you love, my love,
to view my love for you my love –

DOÑA CLARA. *(Crushing the letter.)* Mother of God!

PEPITA. Señora. It is late.

DOÑA MARÍA. Ah, Pepita!

PEPITA. We must go. Or we will miss the curtain.

DON VICENTE. *(Indicating letter.)* May I?

DOÑA CLARA. *(Handing* **DON VICENTE** *the letter.)* It's
yours. You're certain to enjoy it.

UNCLE PIO. Pepita was an orphan raised by that strange
genius, the Abbess Madre María del Pilar directress of
the Convent Santa María Rosa de las Rosas. On only
one occasion did the two great women, Doña María
and Madre María, meet face to face.

(The two women sit facing each other.)

DOÑA MARÍA. Dearest Mother, I am looking for some
bright girl to be my companion. Is it possible you might

have some bright girl like that here in your orphanage, a girl I might borrow? A girl you might lend to me – send to me?

UNCLE PIO. Madre María was a woman of vision. Madre María could envision an age when women would protect women – so she'd collect women in mines, in workrooms, in brothel doorways.

She founded a hospital and soon it was full of sickly women she'd found in those places. Madre María had the kindest of faces.

A very kind face and in general a kind of idealism more like a general than an idealist. Madre María was a genuine realist.

She imagined an age of a women's liberation – *after* her death. And so with agitation she felt the cold breath of old age – and a cold rage not for herself but for the work she'd begun. Who would run her mission? Madre María must make a decision.

MADRE MARÍA. *(Appraising* **DOÑA MARÍA.***)* This grotesque old thing, this Doña María – this burlesque of a thing – I hear she drinks now – and mutters to herself as she putters through town in an old dress.

Nevertheless, why waste her acquaintance. Though she drinks herself blind – where else might I find such a wealthy if unhealthy woman. A woman who might maintain us. A woman who might find my mission worthwhile. A woman who might find we're worth giving to – while I'm living, too. It might be worthwhile to give her Pepita for a little while – let little Pepita live with her – for a little while.

UNCLE PIO. This little thing, this little Pepita –
this beautiful thing of eleven –
the one she saw one day
directing seven other girls at play.

MADRE MARÍA. And later as they laundered the linen, I observed her talent for handling women: correcting the amount of detergent they used – while recounting scenes from the life of St. Rose of Lima infused with a dramatic fire – the means to inspire.

UNCLE PIO. She took her under her wing,
this burgeoning thing,
this little Pepita –

MADRE MARÍA. To complete the work when I am gone.

PEPITA. No one do I love so much as you, Madre María – no place as much as my place with you. Two years I have lived with Doña María. Her maids steal from her – it's hateful. They call her the drunken clod. Two years without you – my dearest Mother in God.

Every day I think of you and pray to hear from you – if I can't be near to you any time soon – but must be on my own. Two years and I am so much alone.

MADRE MARÍA. With Doña María I can give to Pepita the worldly experience of comprehending the worldly, and let her apprehend in the interest of my cause – in the interest of those unprotected by laws.

PEPITA. Some days I fear you have forgotten me. If only you could find a minute to jot me a little letter how much better I would feel. But I know how much you must do.

DOÑA MARÍA.

My dearest
daughter,
there is nothing
I love so much in this
world
as you. I swear
in this no one

PEPITA.

My dearest
Mother in God,
please only a word from
you.
It would inspire
me.

DOÑA MARÍA.
    may call me
    a liar.

DOÑA CLARA.
    please stop
    barraging me with mail –
    you tire
    me. You know how much
    I hate
    feeling I must answer
    when
    I have so many things to
    attend to. I swear I'll
    expire.

DOÑA CLARA.
    Mother dear,

MADRE MARÍA.

    It's late, my dear Pepita –

    and the day has been full.

    I tire now. I must

    retire now.

UNCLE PIO. *(Dispersing the ladies, introducing the young men.)* So much for the ladies.
Now on to these two young men –
orphaned twins – left before
Madre María's convent door.
Twin boys raised by Madre María –
Manuel and Esteban. Heart to heart.
Esteban and Manuel –
Impossible to tell them apart.

They both become scribes,
after learning their letters,
transcribing plays performed for their betters.

(As he makes the stage a theater.) One night, that strange man you know as Uncle Pio...one night that strange Uncle Pio...you'll learn of me later – and the fabulous life I have led. One night – that I was bred a good Castilian... One night... Oh, why wait? I'll simply tell you.

As a kid of ten
I fled to Madrid –
my beautiful mother was dead by then

and my father was glad to be rid of me.

When I got to Madrid I
did what I could to make ends meet:
to earn extra bread
I spread slanders and rumors
for effete nobles with venereal tumors.

At twenty I came to realize three things:
first, my life must be varied, secret and omniscient;
second: I must be near beautiful women –
become for them indispensably efficient.
For I worship beauty, I worship charm –
they torment me of course,
insult me then ask my advice
but I love beautiful women –
I love to see them dressed up –
I love to pin up their hair –
I love each distressing messy affair.
Oh, I love glamorous,
helplessly amorous women.

Third, to be sure,
I must be near those who appreciate the literature
of the stage –
where, by the way,
one meets beautiful women of every age.
And so it was my intention
to combine my ambitions in a single profession.

As a result of some lousy insipid dispute
between a husband and wife
in a run down house of ill repute
my life became too complicated
to remain in Spain. And so I hurled
myself across the sea
to the dominion of Peru –
where after many adventures –

each taking their toll –
I discovered... Camila Perichole

    (**CAMILA** *is there – she acts.*)

who as a matter-of-fact to the well-informed is
the finest actress in the Spanish-speaking world.
She has performed and perfected
dozens of roles I've directed her in –
here in this very theatre
where one night – this very night –
I kindly admit the twin scribes
Manuel and Esteban –
we were dreadfully undersold you understand.

    (**ESTEBAN** *and* **MANUEL** *find their seats, sit.*)

ESTEBAN. Never been to the theatre.

MANUEL. Though we copy the scripts
    for the act-ors.

ESTEBAN. Never entered a theatre.

MANUEL. But deliver the scripts
    to the back doors.

ESTEBAN. Never sat in a theatre –

MANUEL. Never once in a theatre.
    We hear some find the theatre
    intriguing.

ESTEBAN. We are here finding
    each moment fatiguing.

MANUEL. Stories of passion,
    of honor, of love –

ESTEBAN. That fat young woman
    has just dropped her glove
    and is pressing her breast
    against my knee to retrieve it.

MANUEL. Just tell her to leave it.
  All the metaphors –
  women as fountains, women as flowers.

ESTEBAN. We've had women –
  have no doubt – had them for a while
  before going on.

MANUEL. What are they all going on about?

  (CAMILA performs a diverting dance.)

UNCLE PIO. Between the acts, the Perichole
  steps as usual out of her role
  as a countess or a queen,
  puts on twelve petticoats
  and dances in front of the curtain.
  Esteban leaves, but Manuel
  stays in his seat,
  entranced I am certain
  by the Perichole's delicate feet.
  The red stockings of Camila Perichole
  make their impression
  on the young man's soul.

  *(CAMILA "delivers" a serious soliloquy to her
  stage partner – perhaps a king.)*

DOÑA MARÍA. The theatre is charming,
  the theatre is lovely.
  I love to visit the theatre.
  Are you enjoying yourself Pepita?

PEPITA. Oh yes, but please Madam, we should try to keep
  our voices down.

DOÑA MARÍA. The stage stories –
  the actors pretending –
  the characters – you see –
  are mending their ways

for the play is ending.
It's all accomplished with remarkable tact.
In fact, that is the playwright's "art" –
not to offend, not to insult,
not to commend or exult in human folly.

PEPITA. Yes please, but softly Madam, the actors might
hear.

DOÑA MARÍA. Dear, dear. The author here
constructs a play that instructs
us (in a way) how we might
better learn to behave
ourselves. To save
ourselves from some dreadful fate.
If it's not too late.

PEPITA. Madam, please.

DOÑA MARÍA. That is the playwright's chore.
And yet what a bore it all is.
The plot is sagging, the acting is fake,
my attention is flagging,
I can hardly stay awake for goodness sake.
If not for the Perichole's
wit and grace, intelligence,
elegance and command of rhyme,
this spectacle of taste
would be a waste
of everyone's time.

UNCLE PIO. There she stands the star of the show.
Attention is what she demands –
and all in attendance bestow it.

(**CAMILA** *returns to her diverting dance.*)

Between the acts she steps from her role
just long enough to cajole
the crowd with a song or two.

She puts on red tights and sings in a *low* register.
And if anyone is pert enough to shout *"higher"*
she raises her skirt above her knees –

CAMILA. *(Seductively to the audience.)* I love to give pain –
I do as I please.

UNCLE PIO. Tonight – to the delight of those in attendance –
she makes obvious reference
to the Marquesa – our Doña María –
whose eyes were closed
and appeared to have dozed off
during her soliloquy.

CAMILA. *Stingy old slime –*
she reeks of liquor half the time.
Oh the stains on her dress
and her daughter taking flight from her under duress
to Spain. She chatters away – the old pot –
there's even snot running out of her nose.
Do you hear the audience roar?

DOÑA MARÍA. And yet what a bore it all is.
The plot is sagging, the acting is fake,
my attention is flagging,
I can hardly stay awake for goodness sake.
If not for the Perichole's
wit and grace, intelligence,
elegance and command of rhyme,
this spectacle of taste
would be a waste
of everyone's time.

PEPITA. *(To herself.)* The things the actress... How dreadful.
(To **DOÑA MARÍA.**) I think it's time we go, Madam. Let
me lead you to the door.

CAMILA. *Do you hear the audience roar?*
Do you understand?
Are you thinking of your child?
Do you know your child can't stand you?

PEPITA. Madam, this way.

CAMILA. *(After watching them exit. To herself.)* The little
    girl that leads her away...
    They say she's an orphan – eleven or so.
    I was eleven – dear God in heaven –
    when my mother sold me to Uncle Pio.

    My mother who whipped me
    and forced me to sleep in a wine shed.
    Only after she sold me for a piece of gold
    did I sleep in a real bed.

    Mothers or daughters –
    what's there to say?
    They turn you away.
    They turn you away

        *(**MANUEL** is there.)*

MANUEL. Drifting among the trees beneath her dressing
    room window. Drifting among the trees so I might see
    her. Leaning against the trees night after night. In the
    dark I can hear my own loud heart beats.

UNCLE PIO. Manuel has had women –
    have no doubt – had them
    for a while before going on.
    What is he going on about?

MANUEL. Leaning against the dark trees, my knuckles
    between my teeth when I see her lovers arrive, listening
    to my own loud heart beats.

        *(**ESTEBAN** appears.)*

ESTEBAN. My brother's secret – now I know why his
    errands make him go every night past the theatre. He
    hopes to meet her and exchange a word. His groin
    pressed up against a tree as he stares up at her window.

UNCLE PIO. A simpler texture – Esteban's heart – than
    Manuel's – his attachment to his brother is all he

desires. Thus he discovers the secret from which few recover.

That even in the most perfect love –
whether lover or brother –
one person always loves less profoundly
than the other.

MANUEL. Drifting among the trees beneath her dressing room window.

ESTEBAN. Drifting among the trees unseen by my brother.

MANUEL. Drifting among the trees so I might see her.

ESTEBAN. I keep my eyes on him – just as Madre María bade each of us do.

MANUEL & ESTEBAN. Night after night leaning against a tree in the dark I can hear my own loud heart beats.

(Camila's dressing room. She sits, combing her hair, gazing into her mirror.)

CAMILA. Which one are you, Manuel or Esteban? Esteban or Manuel? It is impossible to tell you apart.

MANUEL. Manuel.

CAMILA. It doesn't matter. You are both of you unfriendly. Here I sit all day learning stupid lines from one wretched play or another. Do you look down on me because I am an actress – and because though I speak lines on stage I can neither read nor write? It's true. I learn my words by rote. My Uncle Pio reads them aloud to me. Well, think as you wish.

*(She stands, offers **MANUEL** her seat.)*

(Indicating chair.) Well, don't just stand there – sit.

*(Crossing, her back to **MANUEL**.)* I sent for you because I want to engage you to write a note for me – actually two – two letters – both very secret – demanding discretion. But I see by your expression that you don't

like me – and that to ask you would be as good as reading them aloud from the stage. Are you my friend?

MANUEL. Yes, señora.

CAMILA. Go away. Send me Esteban. You have no affection for me. You do not say *Yes, señora* as a friend would say it.

(After a pause.) Are you still there?

MANUEL. Yes, señora...you can trust me to do anything for you. You can trust –

CAMILA. *(Finally turns to* **MANUEL**, *goes to him.)* You must promise me you will never never mention to any other human being what is in these letters, or even that you wrote them for me.

MANUEL. Yes, señora.

CAMILA. Don't just say *Yes, señora. (Seductively.)* Why are you looking at me like that?

MANUEL. *(Emphatically.)* I swear by Santa María Rosa de las Rosas that I will keep what is between us a secret.

CAMILA. Even from Esteban?

MANUEL. Even from Esteban.

CAMILA. Very well. Now write:

To his Excellency, Don Andrés de Ribera, Viceroy of Peru. Camila Perichole kisses the hands of Your Excellency No tear that up. Write. *To his Excellency, Don Andrés de Ribera, Viceroy of Peru. Michaela Villegas, stage artist kisses the hands of Your Excellency – and says that Your Excellency's suspicion that I would entertain the favors of any other beside Your Excellency (above all a matador) are ridiculous, false and insulting. I return your recent gifts.*

And now the second note:

UNCLE PIO. And here she chastises a famous matador with whom she is sleeping.

CAMILA. *Pedro (Idiot!) how dare you dedicate a bull to me at the stadium! Are you not aware the unwanted attention that brings to our affair? I swear –*

UNCLE PIO. She swears –

CAMILA. *If you do that again I will banish you from my presence. P.S. At the usual place on Friday night.*

(Putting a coin in his hand, holding his hand.) That will be all – there is your money. I shall want you to write for me more of the same from time to time. My Uncle Pio generally writes my letters. These I do not wish him to know about. Good night, sweetheart. Go with God. And go out the way you came.

(DOÑA MARÍA appears.)

DOÑA MARÍA. *(Before a mirror – tipsy.)* I drink on occasion –
I know people know, and so what?
Since my daughter's departure
I traipse through the house
in pretend conversation.
Well, drink's consolation.
But when I write my letters to her
I abstain and remain perfectly sober.
With my missives completed and posted,
I lock myself up – and engaged
in imagined dialogues become so enraged,
I have to get toasted and then...
I begin the whole cycle again.

PEPITA. Madam – a lady – that actress – the one – when you were talking – at least when she sang – I think you didn't hear –

DOÑA MARÍA. My dear child, it would be best if only one of us remained incoherent. And that shall be me. Continue and make yourself clear.

PEPITA. The actress – the one they call the Perichole – she calls with a letter from the Viceroy.

DOÑA MARÍA. Oh, heavens, no. I'm in no state – look at my face – bid her wait in my sitting room. Stay with her there and be nice to Her Grace.

CAMILA. I come señora to make sure that you did not misunderstand anything I said on the evening Your Grace did me the honor to visit my theatre.

(A chair is placed for **DOÑA MARÍA**, *she sits.)*

DOÑA MARÍA. Pepita, please, fetch the lady a chair. Misunderstood? Misunderstood? I dare say, I understood everything you said quite clearly.

CAMILA. Yes of course.

DOÑA MARÍA. Please, sit there.

(The two women sit facing each other.)

CAMILA. And that is why, Your Grace, the Viceroy... Don Andrés.

DOÑA MARÍA. Don Andrés, yes.

CAMILA. Compels me to your door to beg your forgiveness.

DOÑA MARÍA. Forgiveness?

CAMILA. A poor actress in my position may be carried away beyond her intentions. I pray Your Grace did not think my words were intended to offend.

DOÑA MARÍA. Heaven forfend, señora? You gave a beautiful performance that evening. You are a great artist. That soliloquy you spoke near the end of the second act – I shut my eyes to listen – you were sublime.

CAMILA. I thought perhaps you slept –

DOÑA MARÍA. I shut my eyes I say to listen and listen – I nearly wept – your voice kept finding new wonders in the verse. You are a wonder – always – even when the script lacks – as it did that night.

CAMILA. Yes, but it was in the songs…the rhyme between the acts of the comedy. The Viceroy was afraid Your Grace –

DOÑA MARÍA. Yes, yes, that song… I remember now. I'm afraid I did not listen closely to it – though I'm sure you sang it well – I was thinking still of your soliloquy. And then we left early – did we not, Pepita? I can't remember – why did we go? Perhaps I grew tired. I am an old woman, you know.

CAMILA. You are so good to overlook my childishness.

DOÑA MARÍA. Childishness? My gifted child! How could I an unwise and unloved old woman be offended by you? I have been contemplating that speech you rendered so beautifully – the one on the nature of selfless love. Did you know my daughter, Doña Clara?

CAMILA. Her Grace often did me the honor of visiting my theatre. I knew the Condesa well by sight.

DOÑA MARÍA. Do not believe those in town that say she is unkind to me. Think, one day we fell out – I forget over what? We both said hasty things and went off to our rooms – then each turned to be forgiven. Finally, only a door separated us – and there we were pulling it in contrary ways. But at last she…took my…face…thus, in her two white hands – I'm glad you're here to hear from my own lips that she is not unkind to me as some people say. The fault was mine. Look at me. Look at me. There was some mistake that made me the mother of so beautiful… Oh, I am a stupid old woman. Let me kiss your feet.

> *(Dropping to the floor, attempting to kiss* **CAMILA***'s feet.)*

I am difficult. I am trying. I am impossible. I am impossible. *(As* **PEPITA** *leads her away.)* Forgiveness, forgiveness – forgiveness is all I ask – of you – of everybody.

CAMILA. *(Rather shocked.)* Mother of God. Is this what family relations bring us to – family relations we cling to throughout our lives? People we cannot understand – let alone stand them.

UNCLE PIO. Indeed. What drama we make of each other – how deep our desires go?
And what of ourselves – if we choose to inquire?
What in God's name do we know?

ESTEBAN. He continually broods over her – Manuel does. His moods – Manuel's. Today – for the – I don't know how many times before – a boy asked me, Are you Manuel? (Not even Madre María can tell us apart.) I'm Esteban. Well, your brother is wanted by the actress at the theatre.

UNCLE PIO. That night. At midnight – the usual Friday night of Camila's assignations with the bullfighter – Esteban has gone to bed – Manuel stays up by the light of a candle – his head resting in one hand – copying out parts for a motet. A knock on the door –

> *(***CAMILA*** makes a dramatic appearance, sails into the room, veiled, out of breath.)*

CAMILA. It's me.

MANUEL. Señora!

CAMILA. *(Throwing back the veil from her face.)* Quick, ink and paper. You must – a letter for me. Who's there? In the bed – eyes staring at me. *(To* **MANUEL.***)* You're not Esteban are you?

MANUEL. I'm Manuel.

CAMILA. Mother of God, I can't tell which of you is which.

Excuse me Esteban – I know it's late, but it is necessary. Now write this for me, Manuel:

I, the Perichole – I don't know what you take me for – am not accustomed to wait at a rendezvous. Remember – all over Peru there are greater matadors than you my friend. I am half Castilian – and that a million actresses in the world do not compare to me. Underline that. *You shall never have the chance – the opportunity – better – to keep me waiting again.* Underline that. *I shall laugh the last – for even an actress does not grow old as fast as a bullfighter.*

Hurry, write!

MANUEL. It is done.

CAMILA. Here – on the table – a coin – it is yours. Farewell for now.

> (**CAMILA** *exits.*)

MANUEL. *(To himself.)* I worship her. But she's a fiction. A figure on the stage. *(To* **ESTEBAN.***)* Esteban, that's the last letter I write for that woman. She can find another pander. If she calls again, Esteban, or sends for me when I'm not here, make it plain I will have nothing else to do with her.

ESTEBAN. You don't have to say what you just said, Manuel. I don't care whether you write her letters or not. Why did you even tell me?

MANUEL. What are you talking about? What made you think I was saying that for you? Do you think I want to write any more of her dirty letters?

ESTEBAN. You love her. You don't have to change because of me.

MANUEL. *Love* her? *Love* her? You're crazy Esteban. How could you say I love her?

ESTEBAN. You just said you worship her – I heard you.

MANUEL. Yes, but what chance would there be for me? Do you think she'd give me those letters to write if there were any chance? Do you think she'd push a piece of money across the table... You're crazy, Esteban. Go back to bed.

ESTEBAN. I'm going out for a walk.

MANUEL. It's after midnight – and it's raining. Where would you go?

ESTEBAN. I don't know.

MANUEL. Look, Esteban. I'm all right. I swear to you there's nothing left to all that. I don't love her. I only did for a time.

ESTEBAN. I'm in your way.

MANUEL. In the name of God, Esteban, get back in here.

ESTEBAN. Let go of me... Manuel be careful – the metal spike – the door.

UNCLE PIO. Yes, Manuel – perhaps he loves Esteban more profoundly than we imagined – for in pulling his brother back inside with him – in jumping so recklessly – to keep his brother safe – he bumps against a rusty piece of metal on the door tearing open his knee.

Oh, the human heart – oh
the imperfection. Who is wise
enough to recognize
his own frailty? Before we know it
some part of us is bleeding.
Do we realize it's leading
to infection?

One could press on now to another strand of this three-partitioned tale – back to each antic of Doña María or the frantic isolation of Pepita or the fervent aspiration of Madre María. And yet we've hardly touched on my relationship with Camila. There's such a lot to do in interlocking stories.

(The **ACTOR** *playing the various roles now enters.)*

This actor is Don Andrés, the Viceroy of Peru – Camila is his mistress –

DON ANDRÉS. *(In wig, with handkerchief.)* Though not her only lover – and I know it. The son she bore me – Jaime – he's two years old now and has inherited my rickety constitution – prone to the persecution of quakes and fits of epilepsy. Thus far he has been spared my gout.

UNCLE PIO. This actor is also Captain Alvarado – an ocean faring man and friend to Manuel and Esteban.

CAPTAIN ALVARADO. *(Having switched from wig to captains hat.)* Suited as I am to a life wandering the globe – it prevents me pondering the loss of my daughter Estella. I go about the world like a blind man does about an empty house. A life on the water.

UNCLE PIO. Thank you – that was lovely.

(The **ACTOR** *exits.)*

Now where we? Oh yes, deciding whether to stay with Manuel and Esteban – bring it to its pinnacle before the disaster on the bridge. You know of that already – that five of our characters must die. That strain is Wilder's persistent refrain – how death must remain – no matter how we dream away our lives – what are the words and where are they from – that death is constantly to our left until the moment it taps us on the shoulder. We turn our head – and there we are – dead! I paraphrase and I can't recall the source. But you get my point. Oh, let's stick a bit longer with Esteban and Manuel whose infected leg has begun to swell.

ESTEBAN. The doctor – he says we must continue to apply these cloths to your knee.

MANUEL. But every time you apply the ointment it burns and the pain grows worse.

ESTEBAN. All will be well. A day or two, Manuel, and you'll be out and about.

MANUEL. I beg you, my brother, no more of that salve. I can't stand it. *(As* **ESTEBAN** *applies the cloth.)* God condemn your soul to the hottest hell there is. A thousand devils torture you forever Esteban. Goddamn your soul you hear.

ESTEBAN. Be still my brother.

MANUEL. May God damn your beastly soul for coming between us the Perichole and I. She is gone. What right had you –

> *(An instantaneous switch is accomplished by a pivot on the part of* **ESTEBAN.***)*

While I sleep, you say, condemn you to burn because of that woman? That's crazy – you're all I've got. She means nothing to me.

I feel better, Esteban. I'll be up and around tomorrow. But you – you haven't slept for days. Soon I won't cause you any more trouble.

ESTEBAN. It's no trouble, you fool.

MANUEL. You mustn't take me seriously when I try and stop you from putting on the cloths – the ointment burns is all.

ESTEBAN. Don't you think I should send for the Perichole? She could just come and see you for a few minutes...

MANUEL. Are you still thinking about her? I wouldn't have her here for anything.

ESTEBAN. Manuel, you still feel, don't you that I came between you and the Perichole? I told you it was all right with me. I swear to you I'd have been glad if you'd gone away with her.

MANUEL. Why are you bringing that up? She's nothing to me now. It has been burned out of my system. Forget about it.

ESTEBAN. Manuel, I wouldn't speak of it, only when you get angry with me about the cloths and the ointment – you talk about it and you –

MANUEL. Look, I'm not responsible for what I say then. My leg hurts then, that's all.

ESTEBAN. Then you don't damn me because it looks like I came between you –

MANUEL. Damn you...? What makes you say that? You're all I've got in the world. You haven't had sleep, Esteban – I've been a curse to you – you're losing your health because of me. But you'll see I won't be trouble to you much more.

ESTEBAN. Let me apply the cloths –

MANUEL. My one chance to love a woman and you stole it from me Esteban. Your soul will dance in flames.

(MANUEL exits, MADRE MARÍA is there.)

MADRE MARÍA. The innkeeper sent for me. Your brother is dead. They say you've been wandering the city – I find you here in the middle of town. I want you to help me. Won't you come back to your lodgings and see your brother? Won't you come and help me? He must be buried. No one knows which of you has died. Even I have never been able to tell you apart. If you won't help me, will you at least tell me which one you are?

ESTEBAN. Manuel.

UNCLE PIO. Esteban says Manuel.

MADRE MARÍA. Manuel, won't you come and sit with me – just for a short time? As children you did so many things for me. You were willing to go across town on some little errand. And when I told you both the story of the crucifixion you jumped up and said if Esteban and I had been there we would have prevented it. I, too, Manuel, have lost. I too...once. We know that God has taken them into His hands... It is so long ago now, and I have never told anyone. Let me tell you.

(MADRE MARÍA steps away, CAMILA appears.)

UNCLE PIO. But he walks away and does not hear her out – so we never know who or what is lost to her.

CAMILA. What is it, Manuel? Why will you not write my letters? Is my money no longer good enough for you? Why do you run away whenever you see me?

(CAMILA walks away, CAPTAIN ALVARADO appears.)

MADRE MARÍA. Since his brother's death, Captain Alvarado, he has drifted a year from province to province. But always he returns to Lima. He is in Cuzco now doing some copying for the University. Please – can you –

(DOÑA MARÍA appears. DOÑA CLARA appears reading the letter.)

DOÑA MARÍA. Captain Alvarado is bringing you this letter in person, my darling one. He is a diamond of sincerity. You will never meet anyone who has travelled so far. One day I asked him why he lived so – and he avoided my question. I discovered from my laundress what I think is the reason for his wandering. My child, he had a child – my daughter, he had a daughter. She was just old enough to –

CAPTAIN ALVARADO. Don't you recognize me? I'm Captain Alvarado – you and your brother once worked for me. Funny running into you here in Cuzco.

ESTEBAN. Yes.

CAPTAIN ALVARADO. I am looking for some strong fellows to go on my next trip with me. Would you like to come? England and Russia. Hard work. Good wages... A long way from Peru. Well?

I said: Do you want to go on my next trip with –

ESTEBAN. Yes. I'll go.

CAPTAIN ALVARADO. Fine. That's fine. I want your brother, too, of course.

ESTEBAN. No.

CAPTAIN ALVARADO. What's the matter? Wouldn't he want to come? Let me ask him myself. Where is he?

ESTEBAN. Dead.

CAPTAIN ALVARADO. Oh, I didn't know. I'm sorry. Which are you? What's your name?

ESTEBAN. Esteban.

UNCLE PIO. He gives the Captain his real name. I have never understood that.

CAPTAIN ALVARADO. When did Manuel die?

ESTEBAN. Oh, just...a few weeks. He hit his knee against something and...just a few weeks ago.

CAPTAIN ALVARADO. Only a few weeks...?

ESTEBAN. On the ship you must give me something to do all the time – I'll do anything. I'll climb and fix ropes – I'll watch all night – because you know I don't sleep so well anymore.

CAPTAIN ALVARADO. I hear you went into a burning building once, Esteban, and pulled someone out.

ESTEBAN. Yes. I didn't get burned or anything. You know, you're not allowed to kill yourself.

CAPTAIN ALVARADO. I know.

ESTEBAN. But if you jump into a burning house to save somebody that wouldn't be killing yourself.

CAPTAIN ALVARADO. No.

ESTEBAN. I want to give a present to Madre María del Pilar before I go away. I want you to give me all my wages before I start so I can buy her a present. I won't need money anywhere we go. She had a serious loss once – she said so. I don't know who it was. Women can't bear that kind of thing like we can. The present isn't only from me.

CAPTAIN ALVARADO. We'll choose something in Lima.

ESTEBAN. No, I'm not coming. I'm not coming after all. It is impossible. I can't go with you. I can't leave Peru.

CAPTAIN ALVARADO. How about the present for Madre María? You're not going to take that away from her? It might mean a lot to her you know.

The ocean is better than Peru. You know Lima and Cuzco and the road. You have nothing more to know about them. It's the ocean you want. Oblivion. As it has been, Esteban, for me, so will the sea be for you. On the boat you'll have something to do every minute. I'll see to that. Go up and get your things and we'll start. I'll wait for you.

> (**ESTEBAN** *gets a chair, places the back legs roughly on the floor.* **CAPTAIN ALVARADO** *hears the chair legs bang on the floor. Looks up.* **ESTEBAN** *places the front legs of the chair quietly on the floor. After a moment he stands on the chair to hang himself.*)

Perhaps it's best. Perhaps I should leave him.

> (**ESTEBAN** *jumps off the chair.* **CAPTAIN ALVARADO** *catches* **ESTEBAN** *in time.*)

ESTEBAN. Go away! Let me be! *(Weeping.)* I am alone, alone, alone.

CAPTAIN ALVARADO. We do what we can, Esteban. We push on. It isn't for long, you know. Time keeps going by. You'll be surprised at the way time passes.

UNCLE PIO. And so they started for Lima. On the way, Esteban reminded Captain Alvarado that they must find a gift for Madre María.

When they reached the famous bridge of San Luis Rey the captain descended to the stream to supervise the passage of some merchandise. Esteban crossed by the bridge and fell with it.

> *(***DOÑA CLARA*** appears, ***DON VICENTE*** stands nearby. ***DOÑA MARÍA*** appears a moment later reading the letter.)*

DOÑA CLARA. My dear mother, the weather has been exhausting – it is impossible to relax. And the fact that every orchard and garden is in bloom only makes it all the more taxing. I could endure flowers if they had no perfume. I therefore write you at less length than usual. I shall not go to Provence this Fall as my child will be born early in October.

DOÑA MARÍA. What child?

DOÑA CLARA. I can hear her now. "What child?"

DOÑA MARÍA. *(Exiting.)* Pepita!

DOÑA CLARA. But it is best, my darling husband, to be casual when informing her. One foresees the exhausting opportunities news of my condition will provide her – and she's sure to abuse the privilege. You'll scold me, but if I could I would withhold tidings from her all together.

Loss of my figure at the start of the season
is reason enough for despair.

The last thing I need is to have her in my hair
as well. She will try to impose herself.
You may suppose if we don't set about to resist it,
she'll persist and insist on an immediate visit.

UNCLE PIO. Is it necessary to occupy the audience with the details of Doña María's new obsession – her daughters confinement? She prays to the Virgin (to whom she ascribes no true influence) with great fervor, scours books and spends hours consulting an herbalist. Every paste and every gum that can be prescribed to ease the pain of a mother to be or ascribed to benefit the child to come is posted post haste to Spain.

DOÑA MARÍA. Come, Pepita, we will make a pilgrimage to Santa María de Cluxambuqua to pray for my child and my expected grandchild. The acres there have been sacred for centuries.

We must cross the bridge of San Luis Rey and ascend into the hills. Let the Virgin and the gods of the Indians and those earthy gods before them carry to my daughter by secret sensation the sincerity of my love.

We are here.

Stay, Pepita, at the inn. I will go to the church myself.

(She walks in prayer and counts beads.)

UNCLE PIO. *(After a time.)* Out of the shadows of the old church – with all its images of grief and pain – she has prayed for hours. She sits now on the steps of this fountain.

DOÑA MARÍA. *(Sitting.)* God, who I can barely believe in, my fingers have grown tired counting beads, and whispering prayers.

UNCLE PIO. Doña María has arranged that any letters from Spain should be brought to her by special messenger. Even now a boy from her farm runs up –

(Delivering the letter.) Señora.

DOÑA MARÍA. *My dearest Mother...*

   *(**DOÑA MARÍA** reads.)*

How brilliantly she wounds me – a virtuosity of giving pain neatly. My only child.

Invalids roam the garden – hawks plunge in the sky – pilgrims from all over Peru cry out for salvation. What will be will be.

PEPITA. *(Writing a letter.) ...but all this is nothing, Madre, if you like me and wish me to stay with Doña María. We have come into the hills to pray for her daughter. Though I never see you I think of you all the time, my dear Mother in God. I want to do only what you want, but if you could let me come back for a few days to the convent, but not if you do not wish it. But I am so lonely and not talking to anyone, and everything. Have you forgotten me? If you could find a minute to write me a little letter or something that I could keep with me at all times...but I know how busy you are...*

(Exiting, leaving her letter behind.) I must see about the Marquesa's dinner.

DOÑA MARÍA. Pepita, I am back.

*(Absentmindedly picking up **PEPITA**'s letter.) ...my dear Mother in God. I want to do only what you want, but if...but not if you do not wish it. But I am so lonely and not talking to anyone... If you could find a minute to write me a little letter...that I could keep with me at all times...but I know how busy you are...*

I thought Christ opposed all tyrants. The good nun commands this girl's soul – with absolute tyranny... Just as I have longed to do with you...oh Clara –

PEPITA. *(Entering.)* Your supper is waiting downstairs my lady.

DOÑA MARÍA. But my child, aren't you going to eat with me?

PEPITA. I thought you would be tired, my lady. I had my supper already. Would you like me to read to you while you are eating?

DOÑA MARÍA. No, you may go to bed if you choose. My dear child, I am sending off a letter to Lima in the morning. If you have one you can enclose it with mine.

PEPITA. No, I have none.

DOÑA MARÍA. *(Showing* **PEPITA** *the letter.)* But my dear, you have one here for Madre María. Wouldn't you –

PEPITA. *(Grabbing the letter.)* No, I'm not going to send it. I've changed my mind.

DOÑA MARÍA. I know she would like a letter from you Pepita. It would make her happy.

PEPITA. No, it was a bad letter. It wasn't a good letter.

DOÑA MARÍA. Why, my dear, I think it was very beautiful. What could have made it a bad letter?

PEPITA. It wasn't brave.

UNCLE PIO. A grotesque old woman sits alone by the fire. In the crackling flames dance scenes from the play of her life. Her mother's reprimand, her father's rejection, her attempts to command her own daughter's love, her daughter's defection. She hears the smitten girl tearing up her letter – a little girl that begs for love. This old woman who has written so many *exquisite* letters.

DOÑA MARÍA. But all of them are false, are they not? Everything I've ever written. Despite the details...the observations, the wit I've acquired through years of reading and feeding myself on the theatre. I have never brought courage to either life or love. I have grown tired of myself.

A stupid old woman presses pen to paper. How many times has this old crone demanded her daughter tell her how much she loves her? Her alone!

My daughter, I have never...

(She writes in silence as **DOÑA CLARA** *reads the letter –* **DON VICENTE** *standing at her side.)*

(Continues writing.) It is almost dawn, my love. The great tiers of stars glitter above the Andes. She sleeps still – this brave little girl. Do you think she will mind if I brush the damp hair from her face? If only you could see her my darling Clara. This little thing. This little Pepita.

*(***DOÑA CLARA*** *handing pensively the letter to her husband.)*

DON VICENTE. *(Reading the letter aloud.) This little thing of fourteen. A girl who was abandoned – left crying in a puddle of mud. All along, my dear, there was someone beside me dying for love. Always among us there are people we could love. If only we can learn...*

DOÑA MARÍA. *The stars fade. The day encroaches.*

(She puts down her pen.) Let me live now. Let me begin again.

UNCLE PIO. Two days later Doña María and Pepita started back to Lima and while crossing the Bridge of San Luis Rey the accident which we know of befell them.

DON VICENTE. I am the Conde Vicente d'Abuirre, I'm Doña Clara's husband – and son-in-law of the Marquesa de Montemayor.

UNCLE PIO. In the novel *The Bridge of San Luis Rey* he is only referred to –

DON VICENTE. Yet here I am in the play and speeches are conferred upon me. I find the playwright kind and generous indeed! And I thank him for each and every word.

UNCLE PIO. You are most welcome.

DON VICENTE. Now I want to read to you one of Doña María's letters. Her eye for detail and verity of character is one reason I derive such pleasure from her writing and contrive to treasure it for posterity. It will serve as an introduction to this part of the drama.

My darling daughter –

> (**DOÑA MARÍA** *appears.*)

DOÑA MARÍA. *Uncle Pio is the most delightful man in the world – your husband excepted.*

> (**DON VICENTE** *– a gesture of Thanks.* **UNCLE PIO** *– a gesture of Of course.*)

DON VICENTE. *His conversation –*

DOÑA MARÍA. *Is enchanting. If he weren't so disreputable I should make him my secretary. Alas, however, he is so moth-eaten by disease and by bad company that I must leave him to his underworld. I suspect you know to what I allude.*

DON VICENTE. She alludes?

UNCLE PIO. *(Suggestively.)* I leave that to your imagination.

DON VICENTE. *He is like a soiled deck of cards. But what divine Spanish he speaks and what exquisite things he says with it!*

DOÑA MARÍA. *That's what one gets from hanging around a theatre and hearing actors intone the conversation of Calderón.*

UNCLE PIO. Thank you both.

> *(They are gone.)*

We're now going to look in on my relationship with Camila Perichole and we'll begin with a scene in the Perichole's dressing room after a performance. She has played "brilliantly." And as usual the audience is electrified. She returns to find me reading – a sure sign that I'm dissatisfied.

(Camila's dressing room. **UNCLE PIO** *sits, reads. After a moment,* **CAMILA** *returns from the stage.)*

CAMILA. Now what is it? Mother of God, Mother of God, what is it now?

UNCLE PIO. Nothing, little pearl. My little Camila of Camilas. Nothing.

CAMILA. There was something you didn't like. Well, tell me. Tell me.

UNCLE PIO. No, my little fish – my adorable morning star. I suppose you did as well as you could.

*(***UNCLE PIO*** reads.)*

CAMILA. I wish I had never known you – that you had never come into my life – never bought me from my mother. You poison my entire existence. You just *think* I did badly. It pleases you to pretend that I was bad. Fine, be quiet if you wish.

*(***UNCLE PIO*** reads.)*

The fact is I know I was weak tonight – I don't need you to tell me. I don't want to see you around here any longer – I've gotten everything I can from you. It's hard enough to play that part without coming backstage and finding you this way.

UNCLE PIO. *(With his face in the book.)* Why did you take that speech to the prisoner so fast?

CAMILA. Oh God, let me die in peace! One day you tell me to go faster – the next day you tell me go slower. I'll go crazy in a year or two – and then it won't matter.

(Sits before her mirror...busying herself...) Besides, the audience loved it. They loved what I did – they love me – they applauded as never before. Do you hear? As never before! Too fast or too slow is nothing to

them. They wept! I was divine! That's all I care about. Go on – tell me otherwise!

> (**UNCLE PIO** *is silent.* **CAMILA** *suddenly stands wielding a hairbrush – as if she were ready to hurl it at* **UNCLE PIO.**)

You may comb my hair, but if you criticize, I swear – I swear – I'll hurt you. And I'll walk out of this theatre and never come back. You can find some other girl to torture.

> (*She sits, hands him a comb. He stands behind her, combs her hair, hums. Gazes at her in the mirror, combs her hair soothingly for a moment or two. She begins to sob.*)

(*Looking at him as though in the mirror.*) Uncle Pio was I really so bad? Was I a disgrace to you? Was it so awful you left the theatre?

UNCLE PIO. (*Looking at her as though in the mirror.*) You were pretty good in the scene on the ship.

CAMILA. But I've been better, haven't I, Uncle Pio?

UNCLE PIO. You were very good in the final scene.

CAMILA. Was I?

UNCLE PIO. But my flower, my pearl, what was going on in the speech to the prisoner?

> (**CAMILA** *flings herself onto her dressing table caught up in fits of weeping. She then stops.*)

CAMILA. (*Quietly, looking at her reflection.*) Only perfection will do. Only perfection. And that will never come.

UNCLE PIO. Then in a low voice – having broken her down, I talk of the play – analyzing the way it should go. We enter a world of speech, gesture, tempo, texture and rhythm. Camila follows me closely word by word.

There until dawn together alone,
with the lordly conversation of Calderón.

In time, however, as she grew older and her love affairs
took on a bolder contour, Camila lost the absorption in
her art.

CAMILA. Actors and actresses what do we want for
the most part: attention. And for those of us whose
intention it is to achieve it – unless we hold what Uncle
Pio calls the artist's inclination – seek compensation by
other means. That at least is my contention.

DON ANDRÉS. You are a fraud my love. You voice disdain
for the stage until an actress half your age enters the
company. That is what Uncle Pio tells me.

UNCLE PIO. It is true, my lord. Without resorting to
tricks or false inflection, she sets herself to efface
every newcomer. If the play is a comedy she is the very
abstraction of wit. If we place tragedy on the bill, the
stage fairly smolders with rage and the graver emotions.

But such occasions become less and less frequent. Her
technique, to be sure, has become more piquant – but
to my mind she does not conceive sincerity a necessity.
The audience does not notice, but I grieve.

CAMILA. And with that, I take my leave. I've had enough
talk of the theatre. I performed from four this afternoon
until ten at night. Here it is two in the morning.

DON ANDRÉS. Stay my pet. We will suppress conference
on your art. Uncle Pio is on the verge of departure. We
two shall embark upon more intimate congress.

(**DON ANDRÉS** *and* **CAMILA** *exit.*)

UNCLE PIO. We must bump ahead now in our little play.
Scenes, which on the page one would never dream
delete, seem on the stage to defeat the drama. How we
read and how we hear are I fear very different affairs.

We must to the climactic scenes make haste. We've no time to waste in secondary episodes.

Camila's liaison with Don Andrés, which I encouraged so that she might acquire a manner on stage more delectable, has run its course, but not before she developed an unhealthy desire to be wealthy and respectable.

With riches procured from her admirer's favors she secures a villa in the shady hills outside of Cuzco – and fashions herself a lady. She becomes impatient with acting – refers to it as a pastime. And at the age of thirty – with a patina of piety – gives up the stage for society.

A middle-aged woman who was once an actress walks through her gardens and talks with her young son. It's five years since she retired – attired now in jewels and plumes. She's learned to read and write more or less – now that she no longer needs to shout from the stage, and consorts with noble fools and tries to assuage the feeling that her life is meaningless. She wonders when the felicity she assumed would be hers with social position will be written on her heart. When, she asks herself daily, will my new life start?

(*The* **ACTOR** *manages the puppet representing* **JAIME**.)

JAIME. What, Mother?

UNCLE PIO. That's her little son, Jaime. Her child with Don Andrés.

CAMILA. Nothing, sweetheart.

UNCLE PIO. He's epileptic – her child – like his father. You might think someone as vain as Camila would have little tolerance for the pain of this grave and serious boy. But she is patient. He is her joy.

CAMILA. Go Jaime – into supper.

JAIME. Good-night Uncle Pio.

UNCLE PIO. Good-night my son.

*(The **ACTOR** exits with the puppet.)*

CAMILA. I'm late, I'm sorry. What is it you wish to say to me?

UNCLE PIO. Camila –

CAMILA. My name is Doña Micaela. I was born Micaela Villegas. I am now Doña Micaela.

UNCLE PIO. I do not wish to offend you, Doña Micaela, but as you let me call you Camila for twenty years, I should think –

CAMILA. Oh, do as you like. Do as you like.

UNCLE PIO. Camila, promise me you will listen to me and not run away at my first sentence.

CAMILA. Uncle Pio, listen to me. You are mad if you think you can make me return to the theatre. I look back at that life with horror. You are wasting your time.

UNCLE PIO. I would not have you come back if you are so happy with these new friends.

CAMILA. If you don't like my new friends, then go. The years of your correcting me are over. I don't want any advice. Stop directing me.

It will be cold in a moment. I must go back into the house.

UNCLE PIO. Dearest Camila, please, suffer me ten minutes. You never come to see the theatre – the audiences are falling away. They only put on the Old Comedy twice a week – all the other nights are the new farces in prose. All of it is so dull and indecent. No one speaks properly. No one can even walk properly on the stage. It is shameful.

CAMILA. Forgive me Uncle Pio, for being so rude to you. Jaime was ill this afternoon. He is so ashamed when the epilepsy comes in public – he feels degraded.

It would be no good if I went back to the theatre. The audiences come for the spectacle now – for the prosaic farce – you just said so. We were foolish to try keeping alive the old style. It is not worth fighting the crowd.

UNCLE PIO. I was not fair to you when you were on the stage. I begrudged you the praise you deserved. You have always been a great artist. If you come to see that you are unhappy among these people you might think of us going to Madrid. You would have a great triumph there. You are still young and beautiful. There will be time later to be called Doña Micaela. We shall be old soon. We shall be dead soon.

CAMILA. No, I shall never see Spain. All the world is alike – Madrid or Lima.

UNCLE PIO. Oh, if only we could go away to some island where people would know you for yourself and love you. *(Filled with emotion.)* Of course I love you as I always must – and more than I can say. To have known you is enough for my whole life.

CAMILA. *(Smiling fondly, her heart breaking.)* How absurd you are. You are fifty years old, yet you say that as a boy would – your big ridiculous eyes. There is no such thing as love of that kind – or that kind of island. It is only in the theatre that you find such things.

It's growing cold. You must be resigned. Do not think of me any longer. Just forgive, that's all. Forgive.

(She kisses his fingers and runs away.)

UNCLE PIO. Suddenly the news was all over Lima that the lady that used to be called the Perichole had the smallpox. Her beauty impaired, she leaves the city, retires solely to her villa. She returns the jewels to those that had bestowed them on her. She allows no one but her maids and her child to see her.

DON ANDRÉS. As answer to my repeated inquiries, Uncle Pio, I receive a large sum of money from her with a letter compounded of all that is bitterness and pride.

CAMILA. *(Appearing veiled.)* Anyone attached to me was so because they thought me beautiful. My face is ravaged. Any further attention paid will spring from pity and condescension. There is no love – only passion and self-interest.

DOÑA CLARA. I hear –

DON VICENTE. From who – your mother?

DOÑA CLARA. No, darling – from others – that she –

DON VICENTE. The actress?

DOÑA CLARA. The Perichole, yes – that she is determined to return more than was ever given her. The poor dear. The approach of poverty compounds the gloom of her isolation. Even that queer Uncle Pio is forsaken by her. He caught her one day by accident in her room smearing the once celebrated face with a paste she created. The effect I suspect was grotesque. The blemishes did not vanish.

And his amazed glance
which she caught by chance
in her glass was enough in essence
to throw her into a violent fit
and banish that ass from her presence.

UNCLE PIO. We move quickly now to the scene months later where I – wounded and bereft of my adopted one – adopt the voice of a girl and lure Camila from her house into the yard.

CAMILA. Who is there? Who is weeping?

UNCLE PIO. Camila, it is I –

CAMILA. Mother of God!

UNCLE PIO. Forgive me, but I must speak with you.

CAMILA. When will I be free of you? Don't you understand? I want to see no one. I don't want to speak to a soul. My life is over.

UNCLE PIO. By our long life together, Camila, grant me one thing, I beg you.

CAMILA. I grant you nothing. Nothing. Stay away from me.

UNCLE PIO. I promise you I shall never trouble you again if you listen to me.

CAMILA. What is it, then? Hurry, it's cold and I am not well.

UNCLE PIO. Camila, let me take Jaime for a year to live with me in Lima. Let me be his teacher. Let me teach him in the Castilian. Here he is left among the servants. He learns nothing. What will become of him? He has a good mind and wants to learn.

CAMILA. Are you mad? He is sick, he is delicate. Your house is a sty.

UNCLE PIO. I have cleaned out my house and apply to Madre María for a housekeeper. As she has given a young girl to Doña María so I think will she give a girl to me. Jaime is in your stables all day. I shall teach him all that a gentleman should know – fencing and Latin and music. We shall read all –

CAMILA. A mother must not be separated from her child. When I was his age – oh, but you know – did not my mother sell me to you for a piece of gold? You are crazy to have thought this up. Give up thinking of me and everything around me. I no longer exist.

UNCLE PIO. *(With desperation.)* Lend me Jaime for one year. I shall love him and teach him as I taught you. Do not let his life –

CAMILA. It is all so meaningless. Meaningless. And I barely have money enough to clothe him properly.

If Jaime wishes to go with you... I shall talk to him in the morning. If he wishes to go with you, you will find him at the Inn about noon. Good-night. Go with God.

UNCLE PIO. Go with God.

(*The* **ACTOR** *appears with* **JAIME**.)

The next day the little boy appears at the Inn I am staying at. He has on fine clothes that are in bad condition. He shows me a small stone his mother had given him that shone in the dark.

(*The* **ACTOR** *places* **JAIME** *on* **UNCLE PIO**'s *shoulders, then steps away.*)

I carry the boy on my shoulders. As we draw near to the bridge of San Luis Rey the boy whispers something about being tired. He is not tired. He is concealing his shame – he knows a fit of the epilepsy is coming on.

I overtake a friend of mine – Alvarado!

CAPTAIN ALVARADO. Ah, Uncle Pio! I must descend to the valley to oversee the handling of some merchandise.

UNCLE PIO. And just as we get to the bridge Jaime speaks to an old lady who is traveling with a young girl. The young scribe stands in the middle of the bridge, aloof and alone. As we approach the mid-point of the bridge I tell Jaime – When we have finished crossing we will sit down and rest for a while. But that turns out not to be necessary.

DON ANDRÉS. A funeral in this heat – I'm a nervous wreck – and I feel ill. Still, I know the crowd will expect me to kneel by each casket and play the father who has lost his only son – choking back a tear or two. I feel I *am* choking. I can't remember the last time I had to go so long without smoking. Captain Alvarado.

CAPTAIN ALVARADO. Your Excellency.

> *(To himself.)* Each and every freak – wishes to steal a peek at the five and those of us that survive them. Candles and incense. It incenses me. How false, how unreal. Estella – my own girl. My dear daughter. Happy are the drowned.

> *(**MADRE MARÍA** appears.)*

UNCLE PIO. An aging woman sits in the Cathedral behind the screen reserved for those who have taken the vow. Now is her heart rent. This aging nun who spent the whole of last evening tearing an idol from her soul.

MADRE MARÍA. It is of no concern if the work I do outlives me. It is enough to work. There is no Pepita now to enlarge my effort. It will expire. Oh hear the long tender curve the soprano lifts in the Kyrie. My affection should have been more of that color, Pepita. It is enough just to serve. The grandeur of my plans makes me dizzy. Dear God in heaven, I have been too busy.

> *(**CAMILA** appears. She remains veiled.)*

UNCLE PIO. And as her head droops Camila Perichole stoops in prayer – at the shrine of the little church outside Cuzco.

CAMILA. I wait for some emotion but feel nothing. I have no heart. I am meaningless. I never offered courage to my son in his sufferings – I held back aloof. And to Uncle Pio I offered no proof of my affection and gratitude. I have failed everybody. They have loved me and I have failed them.

UNCLE PIO. We must let a year pass. Oh yes, my friends, a year. One day Camila hears by accident of the Abbess who had lost two persons she loved in the accident.

CAMILA. But what could she say to me? She would not believe such a person as I could love or lose. What a homely old face she has – it frightens me a bit. Yet day after day I fall humbly in love with it.

Mother... I... I –

MADRE MARÍA. Do I know you, my daughter?

CAMILA. *(Lifting her veil.)* I was the actress. I was the Perichole.

MADRE MARÍA. Oh, yes. I have wished to know you for a long while – but I was told you did not wish to be seen. You too, I know, lost in the fall of the bridge.

CAMILA. You have but to say and I feel again the attack of pain. I cannot reach the hands of the dead. They slip away and I cannot grab hold of them. Mother, what shall I do? I am alone. I have nothing in the world.

MADRE MARÍA. My daughter, it is warm here. It is cooler in the garden. You can rest there. *(As they travel.)* I have wished to know you for a long while, señora. Even before the accident I had wished much to know you. I was told that you were a very great and beautiful actress in the religious plays – in *Belshazzar's Feast*.

(*They are seated.*)

CAMILA. Oh, Mother, you must not say that. I am a sinner. You must not say that.

MADRE MARÍA. We have a beautiful garden – do you not think so? You will come and see us often, and some day you must meet Sister Juana who is our chief gardener. Before she entered religion she had never seen a garden, for she worked in the mines high up in the mountains. Now everything grows under her hand.

A year has gone by, señora, since our accident. I lost two – a young man and a little girl – who had been children in my orphanage. But you lost a real child of your own.

CAMILA. Yes, Mother.

MADRE MARÍA. And a great friend?

CAMILA. Yes, Mother.

MADRE MARÍA. Tell me...

UNCLE PIO. Now Wilder does not give Camila a speech here and it is well beyond my powers – and perhaps unnecessary. So I will leave it. Only, you see, that the whole tide of Camila's long despair – despair since her girlhood when she slept unloved in her mother's musty wine shed found rest in the sun as she wept on the dusty lap of the old nun.

Let's let more time pass and for fun let our versatile friend take on the role of a young nun.

INEZ. *(From offstage, then running on.)* Madre! The Condesa d'Abuir wishes to see you.

MADRE MARÍA. Who is she, Inez?

INEZ. She has just come from Spain. I don't know!

MADRE MARÍA. Oh, this is money Inez – I sense it – our home for the blind. Quick, bid her come in.

> *(INEZ gestures. DOÑA CLARA enters. INEZ exits.)*

DOÑA CLARA. *(After a moment.)* Are you busy, dear Mother? May I talk to you for a while?

MADRE MARÍA. I am quite free, my daughter. Excuse an old woman's memory, have I known you before?

DOÑA CLARA. My mother was the Marquesa de Montemayor. I feel I should not encroach upon your presence before I make a long defense of my mother – who I suspect you did not admire.

This is a page from my mother's last letter to me. She mentions you.

> *(MADRE MARÍA reads.)*

MADRE MARÍA. It is a beautiful letter.

DOÑA CLARA. *(Moved.)* In truth I never knew how to love her.

MADRE MARÍA. *(To herself.)* The day I agreed to give her Pepita. The entire interview I spent thinking such vile things of her. Now learn, learn at last that anywhere you may expect grace.

(To **DOÑA CLARA.***)* I must tell you of Pepita and Esteban – and the Perichole's little son, Jaime – and a rather strange disreputable friend of the actress – a lovable man.

All of us have failed, I fear. One wishes my dear to be punished. One is willing to assume all kinds of penance. But do you know, my daughter, that in love – I scarcely dare say it – but in love our very mistakes don't seem to be able to last long?

Will you do me the kindness my daughter and permit me to show you my work?

UNCLE PIO. A tall, rather languorous beauty from whom the languor has fallen away follows the old abbess who lantern in hand leads her down the corridors of the old convent. This glamorous lady sees the old and young, the sick and blind, but most of all she sees the tired, bright old woman who is leading her.

MADRE MARÍA. I can't help thinking that something could be done for the deaf and dumb. It seems to me that some patient person could... could study out a language for them. There are hundreds and hundreds in Peru. Has anyone in Spain found a way for this? Well some day they will.

DOÑA CLARA. I do not know – but perhaps when I return –

MADRE MARÍA. Do you know, I keep thinking something can be done for the insane. Some day back in Spain, if you hear of anything that would help us, will you write me a letter – if you are not too busy? I am old and cannot go where these things are talked about, but I watch them – and it sometimes seems to me there is a secret about it, just hidden from us, just around the corner.

DOÑA CLARA. I will keep my ears attuned. Surely someone must be –

MADRE MARÍA. Excellent. Now you will excuse me. I must go into the room of the very sick and say a few words for them to think about when they cannot sleep. I will not ask you to come with me there, for you are not accustomed to such...such sounds and things. And besides, I talk to them as one talks to children.

DOÑA CLARA. *(To herself, abstractly.)* All those whom the world has abandoned...that a way is found out to take them in...

MADRE MARÍA. Ah, before I go – this is one of my helpers who had likewise been involved in the affair of the bridge and who had formerly been an actress. Perhaps you know each other?

*(**CAMILA** is there. She is not veiled.)*

CAMILA. Your grace. *(After a moment.)* My face has changed.

DOÑA CLARA. *(Recognizing her.)* Of course...

MADRE MARÍA. She is going out for some of our work across the city and when I have spoken here I must leave you both, for the flour broker will not wait for me, and our argument will be endless.

CAMILA. The Abbess talks to those who are so ill – some of them will not live out the night.

UNCLE PIO. What Camila says is true – all of those in the dark who have no one to turn to – for whom the world perhaps is more difficult and without meaning.

But even as she speaks to those who lay dying, other thoughts are passing through her mind.

MADRE MARÍA. Even now almost no one remembers Esteban and Pepita but myself. Camila alone remembers her Uncle Pio and her little son. And this woman – this Condesa – how many beside her remember her mother?

Soon we shall die and all memory of those five – and of Manuel – will have left the earth, and we ourselves shall be loved for a while and forgotten.

UNCLE PIO. But you know, the love will have been enough. All those impulses of love return to the love that made them. Even memory is not necessary for love. There is a land of the living and a land of the dead and the bridge is love – the only survival, the only meaning.

End

CPSIA information can be obtained
at www.ICGtesting.com
Printed in the USA
BVHW040246160322
631612BV00013B/705